SUPER DC HEROES

THE DARK KNIGHT ™

THE PENGUIN'S CRIME WAVE

WRITTEN BY
LAURIE S. SUTTON

ILLUSTRATED BY
LUCIANO VECCHIO

BATMAN CREATED BY BOB KANE

STONE ARCH BOOKS
a capstone imprint

PUBLISHED BY STONE ARCH BOOKS IN 2013
A CAPSTONE IMPRINT
1710 ROE CREST DRIVE
NORTH MANKATO, MN 56003
WWW.CAPSTONEPUB.COM

STAR28375

CATALOGING-IN-PUBLICATION DATA IS AVAILABLE AT THE
LIBRARY OF CONGRESS WEBSITE.

ISBN: 978-1-4342-4485-7 (LIBRARY BINDING)
ISBN: 978-1-4342-4825-1 (PAPERBACK)

SUMMARY: THE PENGUIN IS ON THE LOOSE... AT SEA! HE'S
HIJACKING HIGH-CLASS YACHTS WITH HIS PENGUIN-SHAPED
SUBMARINE. TO STOP HIM, THE DARK KNIGHT WILL NEED TO
SINK TO THIS SUPER-VILLAIN'S EVIL DEPTHS, OR BECOME
VICTIM TO THE FEATHERED FELON'S FOUL PLAY.

ART DIRECTOR: BOB LENTZ
DESIGNER: BRANN GARVEY

PRINTED IN THE UNITED STATES OF AMERICA
IN NORTH MANKATO, MINNESOTA.
092012   006933CG613

WHILE STILL A BOY, BRUCE WAYNE WITNESSED THE BRUTAL MURDER OF HIS PARENTS. THE TRAGIC EVENT CHANGED THE YOUNG BILLIONAIRE FOREVER. BRUCE VOWED TO RID GOTHAM CITY OF EVIL AND KEEP ITS PEOPLE SAFE FROM CRIME. AFTER YEARS OF TRAINING HIS BODY AND MIND, HE DONNED A NEW UNIFORM AND A NEW IDENTITY.

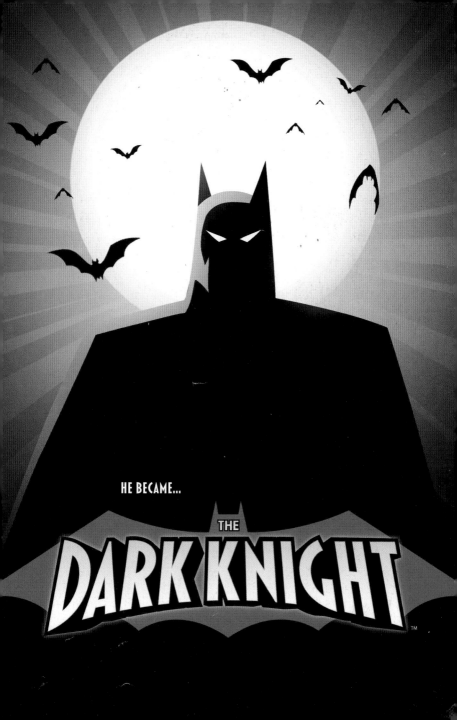

CHAPTER 1

MIDNIGHT IN THE MUSEUM

Batman stood as still as a statue. All around him the real statues were shadowy shapes in the museum. The Dark Knight blended right in.

The Caped Crusader did not move a muscle. He had trained himself to stay in one spot for as long as it took to catch a criminal.

If he had an itch, he did not scratch it. If he had to sneeze, he suppressed it. If he had to breathe, he inhaled as quietly as a bat.

There was a reason Batman stood in the midnight shadows of the Gotham City Museum of Natural History. There was a very special exhibit of rare and valuable fossils on display that were worth millions of dollars. The money was a temptation for any of the super-villains in Gotham City, but one of the fossils was extra special: a skeleton of a prehistoric penguin.

The skeleton was the only one known to exist. Batman knew this was an irresistible lure to the master criminal known as the Penguin. The short and stout villain had a special liking for anything to do with the portly birds. He dressed in a tuxedo to imitate an Emperor penguin. His nose was long and pointed just like a penguin's beak. Even his laugh sounded like a penguin squawking.

WAAUK! came a sound at the entrance of the exhibit hall.

Batman shifted his eyes — but not his head — in that direction. He saw four dark shapes moving into the hall. One of the shapes was very short. It waddled on stubby legs and was supported by an umbrella.

"*WAAUK! WAAUK!*" The Penguin cried. "There it is! Oh, it's such a wonderful sight!"

The villain's attention was focused on a fossilized skeleton. He rushed right past the hidden Batman. The Penguin looked at the ancient bones with admiration in his eyes.

CLAP! CLAP! CLAP!

He clapped his hands together in delight.

"There it is — a *Waimanu manneringi*," the Penguin said. "It's the oldest known penguin in Earth's history." The plump villain sighed in appreciation. "It dates from the Middle Paleocene period, at least sixty million years ago. Isn't it beautiful?"

One of the Penguin's helpers tilted his head. He and his companions were dressed in tuxedos and wore masks shaped like penguin heads. "A why-man-new . . . what?" he asked.

"It's awfully big," another helper added. "I thought all penguins were really small."

The Penguin shot his thug a harsh look. "Oops! Sorry, boss," the thug said.

The Penguin ignored the comment. He knew he was short. He had been teased about it all his life.

"This specimen is five feet tall," the master criminal said proudly. "It was a giant compared to its brethren!"

At that moment, the Penguin realized he should be more concerned with stealing the fossil bones than about defending his own physical stature. "Wrap up this precious prize," he ordered. "I have a special place for it in my collection."

The masked minions obeyed their boss. They pulled out spray-foam guns from their tuxedo jackets and aimed the nozzles at the fossil bones. Their fingers started to squeeze the triggers.

FLAP! FLAP! FLAP! Something gigantic flew out of the shadows. The frightened thieves dropped the foam guns as bat-shaped objects struck the weapons.

"*AWWWK!*" the Penguin squawked.

The shape swooped over their heads. It landed between the Penguin and the fossil and then stood like a dark guardian. Huge bat wings spread out on both sides of its body.

"You're so predictable," the Dark Knight said. "I knew this penguin fossil would bring you out of hiding — and right into my hands."

"Batman!" the Penguin cried. He was not prepared to face his old enemy. "Why don't you get a day job?"

"Crime never sleeps," Batman stated. "And neither do I."

"If you can't sleep, then I've got a way to knock you out — permanently," the Penguin said.

The Penguin turned to his masked helpers and ordered them to attack. "Bash this bothersome bat!"

The costumed crooks rushed toward Batman. "So predictable," said the hero.

The Dark Knight stood completely still and let them come. In the few seconds it took for them to reach him, Batman observed how his opponents moved. He detected their weaknesses and physical faults.

The first one had a slight limp in his left leg that was probably from an old injury. It was an obvious weak spot.

Another thug held his mask onto his face with one hand. That meant it was loose, and the villain could not see through the eyeholes very well.

The third thug was very slow and lagged behind the others. He was hesitating because he was afraid. Afraid of Batman.

The Dark Knight smiled. Fear was his greatest weapon.

Batman launched himself into the air like the creature that inspired his name. He flew straight at his attackers.

KAAAAAAA-POW! Batman's first punch smacked the crook that couldn't see very well. The bad guy crashed to the floor. As Batman expected, the second, limping henchman tripped over the first one and fell to the ground with a *THUD!*

The third frightened crook ran past the spot where Batman had been. He was tempted to keep on running. He hadn't known that the Dark Knight could fly!

What other powers does he have that no one knows about? the frightened crook wondered.

Lost in his fears and thoughts, the crook did not see that Batman was swinging from a Batrope attached to his Utility Belt. **WOOOOOOOOSH!** Batman turned in a huge arc in the air and came back at the startled henchman. To the frightened minion, the Caped Crusader now looked like a giant man-eating monster out of some ancient myth. The thug was frozen with fear.

BLAM! Batman rammed into the crook with both of his boots. The henchman sailed backward and hit the floor hard. He was still conscious, but he didn't get back to his feet. He lay on the ground, covering his head with his hands.

The Dark Knight swooped around in another wide turn. Below him, the Penguin used one of the fallen foam guns on the fossil skeleton. He was encasing the giant penguin in an egg-shaped cocoon.

Batman plunged toward the master criminal like a hawk toward its prey. He snatched the Penguin by the collar of his fancy tuxedo and carried him up and away from the precious fossil bones.

"*AAAAWWWWK!*" the Penguin cried. He still had the foam gun in his hands, so he fired it at his flying captor.

SPLOOOOSH!

The wet goo covered the Caped Crusader's face. But if the Penguin thought the Dark Knight would let him go after that, he was wrong.

Batman tightened his grip. If he couldn't see, it was more important than ever for him to hold on to his captive.

However, the Penguin managed to squirm free of Batman's grasp. "This bird wasn't meant to fly!" he said with a grin.

The portly criminal fell toward the ground. His chubby body hit the floor.

WHOMMMMMP!

Almost all the breath was knocked out of his lungs.

CLACK! CLACK! CLINK!

The foam gun went spinning out of his hands and skittered across the floor, far away from his reach.

The Caped Crusader landed on his feet not far from the Penguin.

Batman slowly scraped the foam from his face and eyes with the back of his hand. When his vision cleared, he saw his foe scrambling for an umbrella.

Batman knew what the Penguin was planning. In one swift motion, Batman pulled out a Batarang from his Utility Belt and threw it. **WOOOOOOOOOOOOSH!**

KLUNK! The weapon hit the umbrella's handle and knocked it out of the criminal's grasp.

As the umbrella hit the ground, the impact activated a sword blade concealed in the tip. **SCHING!**

"It's dangerous to play with sharp objects," Batman said, pointing at the blade. He picked up the foam gun. "Here, let me make it safer for you."

FWOOOOOOSH!

"*WAAAUUHH!*" Penguin squealed as the goo covered him from neck to toe.

"And that's a wrap," Batman concluded.

CHAPTER 2

HIJACKED ON THE HIGH SEAS

When the Penguin told Batman to get a "day job," he didn't know that the Dark Knight already had one.

The Caped Crusader lived two lives. One of them was spent in the dark of night as the world's greatest crime fighter. The other was spent in the light of day as a billionaire businessman named Bruce Wayne.

Keeping those two lives separate and secret was an everyday challenge, but Batman and Bruce found a way.

Until today, when both lives collided.

There was a party going on aboard a luxury yacht anchored in Gotham Bay. The elegant vessel belonged to Bruce Wayne. He was the host of a special celebration. His company was the sponsor of a charity sailboat race. The Wayne World Cup was a race around the world. Each year, the event received international attention.

Bruce and his guests watched the million-dollar sailing yachts compete on the high seas. Live pictures were broadcast from a special Wayne Enterprises satellite.

The race was at a very challenging and dangerous point. The vessels had reached the Antarctic Ocean, the bottom of the world. There, the winds blew without being interrupted by any landmasses. There was a constant current of air at all times.

The wind was a powerful gale at the best of times. At the worst of times, it was potentially fatal.

The party guests watched the action in complete safety aboard Bruce Wayne's yacht. The waters of Gotham Bay were calm. The television screens were large and dynamic. The smallest fleck of sea spray looked larger than life, and the satellite caught every moment with crystal clarity.

KIRRRRRSH! A quick flash of something strange on the high-definition video feed caught Bruce Wayne's attention. The waves didn't look quite right. Batman's crime-fighting instincts didn't shut off when the sun came up in the morning and he took off his cape and cowl. Bruce stood as still as a statue and watched the television screen intently.

Suddenly, a huge shape came up out of the Antarctic waters. *SPLAAAAASSSSH!* The water next to the racing sailboats swelled dramatically. They were nearly tipped over! Bruce and his guests watched anxiously as the crews scrambled to keep the ships from capsizing.

A black-and-white submarine surfaced between two of the sailing yachts. *FOOOOM! FOOOOM!* Harpoons shot out from both sides of the sub and smashed through the hulls of the boats. Then they were reeled in like fish on a line. The other racing vessels sped away from the danger.

Men in black-and-white wetsuits swarmed onto the captured sailboats. The yachts were being hijacked on the high seas! The party guests stood in surprise and watched.

Everyone was motionless with shock. Everyone but Bruce Wayne.

Bruce carefully snuck away from the crowd. Then he jumped into his speedboat and slammed the throttle to full. **VROOOM!** There was no time to waste. He had to get to the Batcave!

Bruce recognized the sub attacking the sailing yachts. It had the shape and markings of a penguin. His old foe was up to new tricks.

It had recently been reported that the Penguin escaped from police custody. That was weeks ago, and no one had seen the crafty criminal. Batman thought the Penguin was simply keeping a low profile in Gotham City. Now it was obvious that the villain wasn't in Gotham at all. He had gone south. *Way* south!

When Bruce reached the Batcave, his faithful butler, Alfred, was waiting for him. He had a change of clothes draped over his arm — a modified version of the Batsuit.

"I thought you would be needing your cold-weather suit, sir," Alfred said. "The Batplane is fully fueled."

"Thank you, Alfred," Bruce said. He took the costume from the loyal servant. "I just have to make one quick call before I leave."

* * *

Soon, the Batplane was in the air and heading south. The flight was going to take many hours, so Batman used the time to search for the Penguin's submarine. The Batplane had all the latest high-tech gear, including links to civilian and military satellites, sonar, and infrared imaging.

The Batplane also had devices that could analyze tiny particles in the air or in the sea. The equipment could even track a butterfly in motion.

The Dark Knight was confident he could find the Penguin. It just might take a while, since the Antarctic was a big place.

* * *

Below the waves of the frigid ocean, the Penguin greeted his captive guests in his custom submarine. They were not feeling very grateful about his hospitality.

"Welcome aboard! You may call me Captain Cobblepot," the Penguin said, using his real name.

"I'll call you Captain crackpot!" one of the sailors replied angrily. "How dare you attack us?!"

"This is piracy!" another man yelled. "You won't get away with it!"

"What do you want?" a female crewmember asked. "A pardon for your crimes? Ransom money?"

The Penguin smiled at her and then bowed. He was dressed in a formal navy uniform from 200 years ago. It was black and white, of course — just like a penguin's appearance. The Penguin was pretending to be a gallant sea adventurer from a long-gone era.

"Ladies and gentlemen, you mistake my hospitality for hostility," the Penguin told them. "You are guests, not prisoners!"

The crew captain stomped up to the Penguin.

"You shot harpoons into our boats and dragged us onto this weird submarine!" the crew captain said. "You bet that's hostile!"

The Penguin shrugged. "I will admit that my invitation was a little out of the ordinary," he replied. He took off his bizarre hat and swished it back and forth like a character in a drama. "But I meant no disrespect. I just like to do things with a little flair!"

"What are you going to do with us?" a woman asked.

"I'm going to entertain you," the Penguin said. "You'll see that I have the highest regard for people of your social standing."

"Not interested," a crewman said.

Another man crossed his arms over his chest. "Me neither," he said.

The Penguin's expression turned from polite to annoyed. These people didn't want to play his game. His pleasant fantasy was shattered.

The villain jammed his antique hat back on his head. "Hmph! You high-society types aren't as civilized as I thought," Penguin complained. "Very well, if you won't play nice, then I'll put you on ice. Take them away!"

Henchmen in wetsuits grabbed the captives and shoved them out of the room. They were marched toward the galley.

"What did he mean he was going to put us on ice?" a worried crewman asked. "Is he going to . . . put us in the refrigerator?"

"Ha!" a sailor scoffed. "That would be warm compared to the weather outside."

The crew people were stuffed into several large cylinders. Layers of frost covered the clear glass. There were three tall tubes and eight sailors, so it was a very tight fit. The Penguin waddled into the galley to watch the panicked looks on their faces.

"I took these devices from Mr. Freeze," the Penguin said.

"What are these things?" the woman stammered.

The Penguin didn't answer her. Instead, he showed her. **CLICK!** He pressed a button on a remote control. **FWOOOOOOOSH!** The cylinders filled with super-cold gas. The captive yacht crews were frozen instantly.

The Penguin grinned. "That will teach you to give me the cold shoulder," he said.

CHAPTER 3

DANGER IN THE DEEP

The Batplane flew over the spot where the sailing yachts had been attacked. The Dark Knight could see the abandoned sailboats drifting on the stormy sea below, but there was no sign of the Penguin's submarine. The infrared scanner did not pick up any trace of engine heat. The satellites did not detect the sub on the surface. The super sonar showed only whales in the area.

Batman knew he needed to widen his search.

FWOOOOOOSH! The strong winds whipped the waves into a white froth. The same winds hit the Batplane like pounding fists. It was a bumpy ride.

Batman struggled to control the plane and keep his eyes on the search instruments at the same time. It was a difficult task, but the Dark Knight was used to being under pressure.

Batman set his focus on his mission and did not let anything else distract him. He was relentless. This was why he was so successful at catching criminals, and had earned the nickname the World's Greatest Detective.

A smear of something dark on the ocean caught his attention. Batman swooped the Batplane into a steep dive. **ZOOOOOOOOOOOOM!**

The aircraft cut through the air like a bullet through the night. It pulled up just above the tips of the waves. There was a black trail of oil floating on the surface of the water.

"It looks like the Penguin's submarine has sprung a leak," Batman concluded.

It didn't take long for the Dark Knight to catch up to the submarine. Even though the vessel was underwater, the instruments on the Batplane still picked up every detail.

PING! PING! The sonar showed its shape and speed on the cockpit screen.

CLICK! CLICK! Infrared satellite images were relayed to the onboard computer monitor. The submarine seemed to be headed straight for a large iceberg not that far ahead.

"The Penguin doesn't know I've found him," Batman said to himself. "I think I'll give him a little clue."

Batman tuned the Batplane's radio to broadcast on a certain band of frequencies. These frequencies were the ones used by the navy that patrolled the Antarctic Ocean. He knew that the Penguin would be listening. After all, the crafty criminal would want to keep track of the authorities.

Batman decided to announce himself. "Attention, Penguin," the Dark Knight said. "I have located your submarine. Surface and surrender."

There was no answer at first, but Batman didn't expect an immediate reply. He could imagine the criminal mastermind being surprised at hearing the voice of Gotham's Caped Crusader way out here.

"Can't a feathered felon swim in peace?" the Penguin responded after a moment. "Leave me alone, you winged bully!"

"You know I can't do that," Batman said. "Not when you attack yachts and kidnap crews."

"I was just trying to make some new friends," the Penguin said. "You know how it is when you move into a new neighborhood. You don't know anyone, and you have to spread your wings a little and meet your neighbors!"

"You are a long way from home," Batman admitted. "But you need to learn how to play nice, or no one will want to be your friend."

"I don't want friends!" the Penguin said. "I just want an audience!"

"It doesn't matter why you committed those crimes," Batman said. "Give yourself up, Penguin, or you'll answer to me."

"I answer to no one! I rule the roost here," the Penguin replied. "In fact, maybe it's time you met some of my subjects."

ZOOOOM! ZOOOOM! A huge flock of black and white robotic penguins headed straight for the Batplane. Batman could see that they wore tiny devices strapped to their heads. They were robots under the control of the Penguin.

"Bye, bye, Batman," the Penguin said. "My little birdies are going to take down the big bad bat once and for all!"

The Penguin hadn't even needed to aim his projectile penguins. The robotic birds homed in on the Batplane's heat signature.

A moment later, the robotic penguins rammed into the plane. *KA·BLAM!* They hit the wings and the engines.

SPUTTER! SPUTTER!

The Batplane lost engine power and started to fall toward the ocean. Batman wrestled with the dying controls.

SNAP! CRACKLE! Sparks popped on the instrument panels. The cockpit filled with smoke. There was no way to keep the plane in the air.

SPLAAAASSSH! The Batplane crashed into the freezing water. The aircraft immediately began to sink, but Batman was not worried. The Batplane was designed to convert into a mini-sub! The Caped Crusader worked the controls, but nothing happened.

"The mechanism must have been shorted out by the bird strike," Batman realized. "I'd better abandon ship."

Batman activated his special cold-weather costume. **FWIPPPPP!** The thermal material heated up and sealed completely around his body. A clear plastic oxygen mask covered his nose and mouth. He could now breathe warm air.

Alfred had been very wise to choose this suit. It would let the Dark Knight survive in the sub-zero conditions of the Antarctic, even underwater.

Batman pulled on the emergency latch to open the cockpit canopy. The clear dome didn't budge. It had been damaged, too!

There was no way for Batman to escape the sinking plane now.

The Dark Knight watched the light from above him slowly grow more and more faint. Then it disappeared. Now there was nothing but blackness all around him. It was like being trapped in a coffin in a watery grave.

THUMP! The Batplane struck something in the dark. It was an underwater ledge. The plane rested on the ridge. Batman was relieved. There was no telling how deep the ocean was around here.

Batman took a pair of pliers from his Utility Belt. "I've got to fix the mini-sub mode before the Penguin escapes," he said.

Even though thousands of pounds of water pressure surrounded him, Batman was not afraid. He had air in the cockpit. He had survival gear and supplies. He had planned ahead for this mission.

The Dark Knight always had a backup plan. He never went into a situation unprepared. In fact, it took a lot to surprise Batman.

However, a gigantic round eye pressing up against the cockpit window came very close to doing just that.

It was at least three feet in diameter, about the size of a truck tire. The eye glowed with an eerie white light. It looked straight at Batman. It did not blink. But neither did the Dark Knight.

That was when Batman saw that the tremendous eye was part of an even bigger body. Suddenly the huge tentacles of a Colossal Antarctic Squid wrapped around the Batplane. Each of the suckers was filled with barbs. *SLURP! SLURP!*

The Dark Knight watched the giant suckers attach to the clear cockpit canopy. They puckered up like a monster's lips.

KTAAAK!

KTAAAK!

KTAAAK!

There was a sharp, cracking sound on the canopy above. For a moment, the Caped Crusader thought the super-hard glass was breaking.

If it shattered, he would be dead in a matter of seconds.

Batman looked around for a split in the canopy. He did not see one.

KTAAAK! KTAAAK!

The sound came again.

Batman realized it was being made by something knocking on the glass!

The Dark Knight turned toward the noise. That's when he saw a face outside in the gloom. It was tucked in between the squid's enormous tentacles. It smiled at the Caped Crusader.

Then a human-shaped hand waved at him. Batman waved back. "Hello, Aquaman," the Dark Knight said.

Aquaman, the King of the Seven Seas, had the ability to breathe underwater at any depth. And the creatures of the ocean obeyed his telepathic commands. Aquaman had sent the colossal squid to keep the Batplane from falling off the ledge. That's why it gripped the Batplane with its tentacles.

Batman gave his friend a thumbs-up signal that meant he was okay. Aquaman returned the hand sign. Then he pointed up. The squid's gigantic tentacles tightened around the aircraft.

WOOOOOOOOOOOSH! They started to surge toward the surface.

CHAPTER 4

UNDERWATER ALLY

Aquaman led the way toward the surface. The giant squid followed, carrying Batman and the Batplane along with it. The creature swam so fast that the Dark Knight's body was pressed back into his seat. He felt as if he were in a rocket being launched into orbit, or riding in some out-of-control, superpowered underwater roller coaster.

It wasn't long before they reached a level where there was some light. Suddenly they stopped.

The squid could not go any higher. Its body was adapted to the crushing pressures of the deep ocean. It could not tolerate the lighter pressure near the surface.

A moment later, Batman saw another dark shape emerge from the darkness. It swam toward them at a slow but steady speed. It was almost as gigantic as the squid.

Then Batman saw it up close — it was a whale! Unfortunately, Batman knew that the whale is the natural enemy of the colossal squid. The remains of Antarctic Colossal Squids had been found in the stomachs of whales. Batman wondered if this whale was just looking for a meal.

But before they reached each other, Aquaman swam toward the enormous ocean mammal.

Aquaman put himself between the potential combatants like a referee in a boxing match. Batman couldn't hear the conversation, but it was obvious that the Sea King was talking to the whale. He pointed at the squid holding the Batplane.

Batman watched the Sea King swim back toward the Batplane. So did the gigantic whale. The squid let go of the aircraft and swam away with a powerful flap of its giant flukes. The Batplane began to sink!

The whale swam under the aircraft and let it settle it upon its back. Then, slowly at first, they began to rise toward the surface again.

Aquaman stood on the wing of the plane as they rose. He nodded at Batman, giving him a thumbs-up.

"It seems like this is a relay team and I'm the baton," Batman said with a grin.

A few minutes later, the Batplane was resting on the snowy surface of a thick, floating ice floe. Aquaman used his sea-strengthened muscles to pop open the stuck canopy latch. Batman jumped out into the cold and greeted his friend warmly.

"Thanks for your help," the Dark Knight said. "I could have been a permanent guest in Davy Jones' locker!"

"I'm glad you called me before you left Gotham City," Aquaman replied. "My finny friends and I are always ready to assist the Caped Crusader."

A nearby dolphin squealed. *EEEEEE! EEEEEE!*

Aquaman nodded at the dolphin.

"He's a big fan of yours," Aquaman said to Batman. Both men chuckled.

A pod of sleek Antarctic Hourglass Dolphins jumped up from the water. **SPLASH! SPLASH!** They were trying to get Aquaman's attention.

Aquaman went over to the edge of the ice floe to listen to the dolphins explain the situation. When he turned back to Batman, he had good news. "My loyal sea subjects have found the Penguin's hideout," the Sea King said. "It's concealed inside an iceberg not far from here."

"Before the Batplane went down, I tracked his sub heading toward a small iceberg," Batman said. "So that makes sense. An iceberg would be the perfect kind of camouflage for the Penguin's underwater vehicle."

"The Penguin was cruel to endanger the animals of the Antarctic," Aquaman declared. "He will answer to me for his crimes against members of my realm."

"He'll pay for *all* of his crimes as soon as I catch him," the Dark Knight agreed. "But to do that, I have to get the Batplane back into the air. I know you're the King of the Sea, but how are you at fixing airplane engines, Aquaman?"

"I'm a better monarch than a mechanic," Aquaman said with a smirk. "But I'll do my best to get your Batplane back up and running!"

* * *

The Penguin's submarine arrived at a dock inside the center of the giant hollow iceberg.

Several other types of ships were tied up on either side of the dock. There were fishing boats, an eco-tourist cruise ship, and even a small navy patrol vessel. The Penguin had played the pirate and taken them from other people.

And now he was holding them for ransom.

Workers in black-and-white snowsuits carried cargo off the boats. The Penguin was taking everything valuable off the ships before selling them back to their owners. Just like the pirates of old, he was plundering the ships.

The kidnapped yacht crew was marched from the penguin-shaped submarine. They had been thawed out and now were going to the brig. This was where all the other captives were kept.

The brig was a prison guarded by large robot penguins with laser rifles inside of their beaks. Their eyes were red and blinked eerily in the dark cavern.

One of the Penguin's henchmen opened the heavy metal door so the new prisoners could enter. He was very surprised when the inmates rushed out. The captives were trying desperately to escape!

The navy patrol captain led the charge. "Take out the robot guards!" he ordered. "Quickly!"

RAT-A-TAT-TAT-TAT! The robotic penguins opened fire with their laser beaks. Beams of super-hot light bounced off the metal prison door and hit the icy walls, making little melted holes that sizzled. However, the navy sailors bravely kept running toward their enemy.

The mechanical penguins were large and dangerous, but they were no match for the onslaught of a hundred determined humans.

"Rip off the heads!" the captain shouted. He grabbed a nearby robot. "We can use the beak guns as weapons!"

BAWHOOOM! Suddenly the whole iceberg shook. Chunks of ice and snow fell from the ceiling. The floor moved sideways under their feet.

THUMP! THA-WUMP! The captives fell flat on their backs. The robot penguins tipped over and powered down.

"What was that?" one of the yacht crew yelled.

"The iceberg is under fire!" another one shouted.

"This whole place could sink!" a sailor exclaimed.

"Let's get to our patrol ship!" the captain in charge cried out.

KA-THUMP! THA-WUMP! In the water beneath the iceberg, Aquaman directed a group of whales to ram the bottom of the Penguin's hideout. He had sent out a telepathic call to humpback whales and even orca. The most powerful creatures of the sea came to carry out his commands.

In the sky above the hideout, Batman circled in the repaired Batplane. He took aim with a small missile.

"Knock, knock," the Dark Knight said. Then he let the explosive weapon fly.

KABLAM! The top of the iceberg blew apart.

Icicles and chunks of packed snow fell into the opening. The Penguin's henchmen and helpers ran away from the docks as the roof caved in. Some of them jumped off the pier and into the water only to face pods of orca sent by Aquaman. The angry whales cornered the men and kept them there.

The Batplane descended into the hollow iceberg using its vertical jets. It came down out of the sky like a giant bird of prey. It was a sight no criminal wanted to see.

The Penguin ran out of the submarine to find out what was happening. After his "guests" had escaped, he had changed back into his tuxedo and top hat. He felt more like himself now.

But when he saw the Batplane landing, he was anything but at ease. He quickly ran back into the submarine.

CLANK! The Penguin locked the hatch.

"That bat has more lives than Catwoman," the portly criminal complained. "The bird strike was supposed to finish him off for good!"

The Penguin ran to the sub's control room. It was empty when he arrived. All his henchmen had run away or been trapped by the whales.

"I always have to do everything myself," he grumbled. He carefully waddled from one set of controls to another, flicking switches and pressing buttons.

VROOOOOOOOOOOOOOM!

The engines rumbled to life and the propeller started to turn.

Outside on the docks, Batman saw the submarine moving.

The Dark Knight saw that it was beginning to pull away from the pier. "Penguin is escaping!" he realized.

CHAPTER 5

THE FINAL FREEZE

"I won't let that bad bird fly the coop," Batman said. He took a Batrope from his Utility Belt. With one perfect toss, Batman lassoed the tail fin of the submarine.

The cold-weather Batsuit protected the Dark Knight from the frigid water as he hauled himself hand-over-hand toward the submarine. He climbed up one of the horizontal stern planes and onto the spine of the ship. When he reached the main hatch, he found that it was locked.

FZZZZZZZZZZZZZZZZT!

The Caped Crusader cut through it with a miniature torch in mere moments.

The Dark Knight jumped down into the sub.

CLAAAANGGGGGGGG!

The sound of his boots hitting the metal deck echoed through the corridors. Batman knew he had to stop the submarine. That meant he had to get to the control room.

There was no one onboard the submarine to stop him. The crew had abandoned ship. When Batman got to the control room, he saw that the Penguin was all by himself.

"Leaving so soon? The excitement is just about to start," Batman said.

"I hate to overstay my welcome," the Penguin replied. "It's bad manners."

"It wouldn't be the same without you. I insist that you stay," Batman said. He threw a Batarang at the instrument panel.

KABLAM!

The controls exploded in a shower of sparks. Immediately, the submarine's engines stopped.

The Penguin had an umbrella hooked over his arm. He always had one with him. To an everyday person, it seemed like it only helped the Penguin walk on his stubby legs. However, the umbrella was also a concealed weapon.

CLICK! The Penguin pulled a trigger in the umbrella handle. A large blade emerged at the tip!

The Penguin lunged at the Dark Knight and slashed at him. Despite being rather plump, the Penguin was very fast on his feet. However, Batman was prepared for this. Quickly, Batman jumped out of the way of the Penguin's strike. **CRUNCH!** The blade plunged into the computer console, destroying one of the monitors.

Batman leaped from place to place in the control room as the Penguin slashed the umbrella knife at him.

SWISH! SWISH!

The Penguin kept missing the Caped Crusader, but kept hitting the instrument panels.

PZAAAK! KZIIIZZZZ!

Soon everything was shorted out or destroyed.

The Penguin gasped. He had worn himself out. When he looked up, he shrieked angrily. "My ship is destroyed!" he said. "Look what you made me do!"

Batman smirked. "All part of the plan," he said. "You're dead in the water, now. Time to surrender."

The Penguin looked defiant at first. Then he dropped the umbrella on the deck, and bowed his head.

"You win," he said meekly.

"I always do," Batman replied. He pulled a pair of Bat-Cuffs from his Utility Belt.

Suddenly the crafty criminal jumped away from the Dark Knight. He snatched off his top hat and pulled an egg out of it.

Despite his extensive knowledge and preparation for the Penguin, even the Dark Knight didn't expect his foe to do something so strange.

The Penguin threw the egg on the deck.

CRACK!

The egg split in half against the floor, spilling out billows of sooty black fumes. Soon, the clouds filled the entire room.

The Penguin used the thick dark clouds to conceal his escape. He snatched up his umbrella and scooted past the Caped Crusader. Then the portly criminal ran from the control room as fast as his stubby legs could carry him.

It was hard for Batman to see, but that did not stop him. The Dark Knight used his other senses to track the Penguin.

CLINK! CLINK! CLINK!

Batman followed the sound of the Penguin's umbrella tip on the metal deck plates.

The sounds led the Dark Knight into the galley. He saw the freezing cylinders there, and instantly recognized them from his many battles with Mr. Freeze. The devices were open and empty.

KA-POWWWWW! Something hit Batman in the back, knocking him into one of the tubes!

SLAM!

The door shut on the Caped Crusader.

HISSSSSSSSSS! Freezing gas hissed into the chamber.

"HAHAHA!" The Penguin laughed.

"I'm going to make a Batman ice sculpture!" the Penguin gloated.

Batman was still as a statue inside the cylinder. The cold air wafted around him, filling the cylinder slowly.

A moment later, the Penguin pressed his face against the frosty glass to gloat over his victory.

Suddenly the door lock exploded. *BOOOOOOOOOM!*

Batman burst out of the freeze chamber and grabbed the Penguin by the collar. Unbeknownst to the Penguin, Batman's thermal Batsuit had protected him from the extreme cold in the chamber. Batman had simply been waiting for the Penguin to get close enough. Now the Dark Knight had his foe by the bow tie!

"**WAAUUG!**" the Penguin said, gasping for breath.

"Is the Hand of Justice too tight?" Batman asked.

"Mercy!" the Penguin gasped.

The Dark Knight was not cruel. He relaxed his grip just a little so that the super-villain could breathe more easily. However, it was just enough for the slippery villain to wriggle free!

CLICK!!

The Penguin pushed a button on his umbrella. Miniature helicopter propellers popped out of the tip.

WHIR·WHIR·WHIR·WHIR! The Penguin held out the spinning blades. "I'll slice you to ribbons!" he cried out.

The Dark Knight rolled backward just in time. He leaped back to his feet, then reached for a weapon in his Utility Belt.

The Penguin tossed an egg grenade at the ceiling of the galley. It stuck to the metal.

TICK! TOCK! BOOOOOM!

Suddenly there was a huge hole in the top of the Penguin's submarine. The Penguin used the helicopter umbrella to fly out of the opening and into the cavern.

"I'm not going to let this bird fly free," the Dark Knight declared.

Batman threw a Batarang with a rope attached out the hole. The rope wrapped around the leg of the Penguin's trousers. Batman held onto the end of the rope, and was lifted out along with the Penguin!

The Penguin dragged the Caped Crusader through the air.

He tried to shake his enemy loose. He swooped and plunged all around the docks inside of the iceberg hideout.

WOOOOSH! They almost hit the side of the navy patrol vessel. **SWISSSSH!** They barely missed the sailing mast of the eco-tourist ship.

"A penguin is a flightless bird," Batman reminded his opponent. "It's time for you to come back to earth."

The Dark Knight pulled sharply on the Batrope attached to the Penguin's pant leg. The force tilted the Penguin in midair and the umbrella propellers tipped sideways. The Penguin and Batman suddenly headed toward the icy water of the docking bay.

Below them, a pod of orca lifted their heads out of the water with their mouths wide open. The Penguin was terrified, and rightly so — penguins were an orca's favorite food!

The fearful felon was shaking so hard that he could not control the umbrella. Batman shifted his weight and guided the umbrella-copter away from the water. A moment later, they landed safely on the snowy ground. The Penguin fell to his knees and kissed the ice.

When he looked up, the Penguin saw that he was surrounded by all the people he had captured. Some of them aimed robot penguin laser beaks at him.

But that didn't make the Penguin cry uncle. He was ready to go on the attack once again.

SSSPLAAASSSSSSSH!

Suddenly an orca burst out of the water and slid on the ice toward the Penguin. Its toothy mouth gaped open. Aquaman rode atop the sea mammal's back like a seafaring cowboy.

"*WAUK!*" the Penguin whimpered. "Please don't hurt me!"

The Sea King stood like a monarch about to issue a royal decree. "You have invaded my realm and harmed my subjects," Aquaman said. "Now you will face my wrath!"

The Penguin covered his head with his hands. "Batman! Save me!" the Penguin begged.

"Gladly," Batman said. He snapped a pair of Bat-Cuffs on the Penguin's wrists.

CLICK-A-CLICK! CLICK-A-CLICK!

"I'm taking you to a nice, safe jail cell," Batman told the Penguin.

"Yes, yes! Just keep that maritime menace away from me!" the Penguin replied. He stared at Aquaman as if the Sea King was a shark.

"Take this sea scum away," Aquaman said. "The sight of him makes me angry."

"Of course, Your Majesty," Batman said to Aquaman. He tried not to smile or chuckle, but Aquaman was playing his royal role to the max. Aquaman nodded knowingly.

It did not take Batman long to put the Penguin into one of the freezing cylinders for the trip back to Gotham City.

When he finished loading it onto the Batplane, he turned to say goodbye to Aquaman.

"Thanks for your help, old friend," Batman said. "It's always good to have a Sea King on my side."

"The King of the Sea and the World's Greatest Detective make a good team," Aquaman said. The two heroes shook hands. Aquaman leaped back into the freezing water as if it were a comfortable bathtub and then climbed onto the back of a waiting orca.

"I'll make sure the captive ships and their crews make it to a safe port," Aquaman promised.

"And I'll make sure this Penguin stays out of hot water!" Batman replied.

THE PENGUIN

REAL NAME:
Oswald Cobblepot

OCCUPATION:
Professional Criminal

BASE:
Iceberg Lounge, Gotham City

HEIGHT:
5 feet, 2 inches

WEIGHT:
175 pounds

EYES:
Blue

HAIR:
Black

Like the flightless fowl he resembles, Oswald Cobblepot has little skill in combat and doesn't seem very threatening. He is, however, a dangerous criminal mastermind constantly in search of easy money. Although he is one of the wealthiest men in Gotham, few of the Penguin's dollar bills have come from honest sources. Expect the Penguin to be protected at all times by a group of hired muscle.

- Cobblepot's waddling walk and beakish nose earned him the unwanted nickname "Penguin." His pursuit of wealth and success comes from the desire to rise above those who have teased him.

- The Penguin operates out of his fashionable nightclub, the Iceberg Lounge, which serves as a safe haven for crafty crooks of all kinds. While there, he spreads his wings in order to connect with the criminal elite.

- The Penguin has a number of tricks up his sleeve. His special umbrellas can hide a variety of deadly tools, including a machine gun, a flamethrower, or a blade. They can also double as a parachute or helicopter, allowing him to fly away from situations gone afoul.

- Penguin has an obsession with birds. He often chooses his crimes so they connect with a bird theme in some way. On more than one occasion, he has used carrier pigeons to send criminal messages.

BIOGRAPHIES

LAURIE S. SUTTON has read comics since she was a kid. She grew up to become an editor for Marvel, DC Comics, Starblaze, and Tekno Comix. She has written *Adam Strange* for DC, *Star Trek: Voyager* for Marvel, plus *Star Trek: Deep Space Nine* and *Witch Hunter* for Malibu Comics. There are long boxes of comics in her closet where there should be clothing and shoes. Laurie has lived all over the world, and currently resides in Florida.

LUCIANO VECCHIO was born in 1982 and currently lives in Buenos Aires, Argentina. With experience in illustration, animation, and comics, his works have been published in the US, Spain, UK, France and Argentina. Credits include *Ben 10* (DC Comics), *Cruel Thing* (Norma), *Unseen Tribe* (Zuda Comics), and *Sentinels* (Drumfish Productions).

GLOSSARY

defiant (di-FYE-uhnt)—if you are defiant, you stand up to someone or to some organization and refuse to obey

formal (FOR-muhl)—proper and not casual

fossil (FOSS-uhl)—the remains or traces of an animal or plant from millions of years ago, preserved as rock

guardian (GAR-dee-uhn)—someone who guards or protects someone or something

imitate (IM-uh-tate)—to copy or mimic someone or something

portly (PORT-lee)—heavy or stout

specimen (SPESS-uh-muhn)—a sample, or an example used to stand for a whole group

subjects (SUHB-jektz)—people who live in a kingdom or under the authority of a king or queen

suppressed (suh-PRESSD)—stopped something from happening, or hid or controlled something

tuxedo (tuhk-SEE-doh)—a man's jacket, usually black with satin lapels, worn with a bow tie for formal occasions

DISCUSSION QUESTIONS

1. Would you rather have Aquaman's ability to command sea creatures, or Batman's many tools, vehicles, and gadgets? Talk about it.

2. Penguin is obsessed with birds. What's your favorite animal? Discuss your answers.

3. This book has ten illustrations. Which one is your favorite? Why?

WRITING PROMPTS

1. Aquaman comes to Batman's rescue. Write about a time when someone helped you out.

2. Penguin commands a team of robotic, laser-beak penguins. Create your own robotic animal companion. What types of attachments does it have? What will you do with your new mechanical sidekick? Write about it.

3. Batman teams up with Aquaman to take down the Penguin. Pick your favorite super hero and write a story about him or her teaming up with Batman. What villain(s) do they fight? You decide!